Because Your Daddy Loves You

by Andrew Clements

◆

Illustrated by R. W. Alley

Clarion Books / New York

Clarion Books
a Houghton Mifflin Company imprint
215 Park Avenue South, New York, NY 10003
Text copyright © 2005 by Andrew Clements
Illustrations copyright © 2005 by R. W. Alley

The illustrations were executed in ink, watercolor, and acrylic.
The text was set in 19-point Tempus Sans

For information about permission to reproduce selections from this book, write to
Permis ons, Houghton   iff in Comp n ,
215 Park Avenue South, New York, NY 10003.

www.houghtonmifflinbooks.com

Printed in Malaysia

Library of Congress Cataloging-in-Publication Data
Clements, Andrew.
Because your daddy loves you / by Andrew Clements ; illustrated by R. W. Alley.
p. cm.
Summary: When things go wrong during a day at the beach, like a ball that drifts away
or a gooey ice cream mess, a father could do a lot of things but always picks the loving one.
ISBN 0-618-00361-4
[1. Fathers and daughters—Fiction. 2. Beaches—Fiction. 3. Love—Fiction.] I. Alley, R. W. (Robert W.), ill. II. Title.
PZ7.C59118Be 2004
[Fic]—dc22   2003013162

ISBN-13: 978-0-618-00361-7
ISBN-10: 0-618-00361-4

TWP 10 9 8 7 6

For my uncle, David Westwood,
one of the best dads ever

—A.C.

For Cassie and Max,
who made me a dad

—R.W.A.

When you wake up from a bad dream and you call out,

Daddy!

Your daddy could say,
Shh! Just go back to sleep.
But he doesn't.

He comes to your room right away
and sits beside you
until you fall asleep again.

8

When the car is packed for the beach
and you can't find your other shoe,
your daddy could say,
You should put things where they belong.
But he doesn't.

He helps you look all over for that shoe.

And when he finds it
under some dirty clothes,
he puts it on your foot
and ties it with a double knot.

When your ball blows across the sand
and into the ocean and starts to drift away,
your daddy could say,
Didn't I tell you not to play too close to the waves?
But he doesn't.

13

He wades out into the cold water.

And he brings your ball back to the beach
and plays roll and catch with you.

When you go for a walk along the beach

16

and you get so tired
that you can't take another step,
your daddy could say,
It's getting late—we've got to keep moving!
But he doesn't.

17

He sits down beside you
and shows you how to make a sandcastle
with a river all around it.

19

When you stop for ice cream on the way home
and your cone makes a big gooey mess,
your daddy could say,
Now look what you've done!
But he doesn't.

20

He finds a paper napkin
and he gets it wet
at the drinking fountain.
He wipes off your mouth,
then both your hands—
one sticky finger
at a time.

When you fall asleep in the car
and it's late when you get home,

your daddy could say,
Hey, wake up! Help me take
all this stuff back into the house.
But he doesn't.

23

First he carries you inside.

And then he goes back
for the toys and the blanket
and the picnic basket.

When you ask for your favorite
story after dinner,
your daddy could say,
We've read that old story
over and over.
But he doesn't.

27

He finds the book,
and he starts at the very beginning,
and he reads every single word.

When you ask for a piggyback ride to bed,
your daddy could say,
Come on, old lazybones, get up those stairs!
But he doesn't.

He swings you onto his back
and marches up and up the stairs,
and drops you gently on your bed,
and kisses you goodnight.

30

And then your daddy could say,
See you tomorrow,
or
Sleep tight,
or
Sweet dreams.
But he doesn't.

31

He says,
"I love you."